The TARTAN TRAMPOLINE and the Pirate

Written by
JENNIFER BAKER

Illustrated by
SARAH CAMPBELL

The Tartan Trampoline and the Pirate

ISBN 978-1-9993668-6-5 (paperback)

Second printing October 2021

Published by
Mòr Media Limited
Argyll, Scotland

www.mormedia.co.uk
Book design by Helen Crossan

Other books in *The Tartan Trampoline* series

The Tartan Trampoline and the Superheroes
The Tartan Trampoline and the Red Shoes

For Antonia Faith

nce there were three children. Manny was the oldest, then came Effie and then Tilly, who was the youngest. All three lived in big busy cities where they went to schools, played in parks and went to shops and museums but, when the holidays came, they packed their bags for the Big Adventure.

They were going to the magic island where their grandmother lived. The journey took them on a train which travelled through mountains and past lochs and sometimes even a ruined castle or two—where queens and kings and princesses and princes lived long ago. At last, they reached the boat that would take them over to the island.

'Hello', shouted the ferryman who was called Allan. (Manny said that he always shouted because he had to be heard above the old engines of the ferry.)

'Are you off to your granny's?'

'Yes,' said Effie, 'but we call her Shayjay.'

3

They didn't know why their grandmother was called Shayjay. She just was. That's a story for another time.

When they got off the boat, Shayjay was waiting for them on the slip.

'Hooray!' she called. 'You're here!'

She gave them all a big hug and bundled them into her car. Shayjay's house wasn't far from the ferry. As they were driving along, Shayjay said, 'I have got a great surprise for you all.'

'What? What?' they all shouted.

'OK, when I shout 'now' I want you to close your eyes … NOW!'
They closed their eyes. Tilly closed hers so tightly they hurt. They heard the car stop.

'Right,' said Shayjay, 'you can open them.'

There, in the field in front of Shayjay's house and right beside the loch, was a huge, beautiful, tartan trampoline.

5

'Oh wow! Can we go? Can we go?'

'Yeah—go!' shouted Shayjay, and the three of them kicked off their shoes and climbed the steps onto the trampoline where they bounced and bounced. They bounced so high that they were nearly as high as Ben Nevis, which is the highest mountain in the land. They bounced till it was nearly dark and Shayjay called them in to eat their dinner.

What with the long journey and all the bouncing, they were pretty tired, so after tea they went to bed in the room at the top of the house, where they could watch the moon and the stars through the window in the roof.

They got into bed quickly and promised each other that whoever wakened first would wake the others so that they could play on the trampoline first thing.

The next morning, however, they all wakened together very early, because the wind was howling round the roof. Sometimes, the wind was so strong on the island that children could not stand up in it and this wind was almost like that.

Manny could remember a Christmas when he was very wee and the waves on the loch were so high that they came over the wall at the end of the field. He remembered that all the grown-ups were worried that the slates would come off the roof or that a tree would fall on the shed but he wasn't worried—he loved it. It made him want to run around and scream and shout. He felt like that on that morning and so did the girls.

They dressed
quickly in lots of
warm clothes and tiptoed down the stairs. They
didn't want to wake Shayjay because they knew she'd make
them stay inside. She'd say it was too dangerous to go out but they
couldn't bear to be in so they opened the door very quietly and
ran out into the field shouting and laughing.

The wind whipped their shouts away
and pulled at their hair and
clothes. It was great!

They climbed up the steps to the big Tartan Trampoline and began to bounce in the wind. They shouted, 'Look—you can see the tops of the mountains!' And then they realised that they were above the mountains—they were actually flying. The wind had picked the trampoline up and was swirling them through the sky.

'Down!' yelled Manny.

And they all lay down on the trampoline, and peered over the edge. It was wonderful. They could see the mountains and lochs and rivers and Shayjay's house, which was like a wee doll's house in the distance.

Suddenly the wind began to drop and gently, gently they came down to rest on an island somewhere in the middle of the loch. It was a beautiful island, with white sands and pink flowers among the sand dunes.

They stepped down from the trampoline and looked around. All was quiet. 'I don't think there's anyone here,' said Effie, her eyes very wide.

'No,' said Tilly. 'I don't think so either.'

But just then—

'WHO ARE YE, AND WHIT ARE YE DAEIN' ON MA TREASURE ISLAND?'

From out of the trees came a very strange-looking man.

'A pirate!' whispered Effie in delight. Pirates are her favourite thing.

The strange man was wearing a pirate's hat but on it was a Scottish saltire instead of a skull and crossbones. He was wearing a pirate's jacket alright, but instead of breeches he wore a kilt which was a bit *too* short. As is the custom with pirates, he only had one leg but that was okay too, because he was using a wooden bottle for the other leg.

Effie looked at him with approval.

'I'm Effie,' she said, 'and this is my brother Manny and my cousin Tilly. Who are you?'

She sounded brave when she said this but, really, she was a bit scared. It had been quite a morning so far, what with the trampoline flying off and then this pirate.

'Ma name is Hamish MacHamish and this is ma island which has treasure which is a' for me so you can jist a' go awa again. An' whit's that?' he said, pointing at the trampoline.

'That's our trampoline,' said Tilly. 'It flies.'

'Where's your treasure?' asked Effie.

14

'It's a' buried so's the likes of you cannae find it.'

'What's the point of that?' asked Manny. 'Don't you want to use it?'

'Aye weel, ah buried it so well, ah cannae find it masel.'

'Have you not got a map with a cross on it that shows you where the treasure's hidden?' asked Effie (she's the pirate expert).

'Och, ah've lost it,' sighed Hamish. 'Ah hud it here in ma sporran an' ah got ma hanky oot tae blaw ma nose an' it wis that windy ah got a' confused. An' then it wisnae there.' He looked very sad.

'We could help you look for it,' said Tilly.

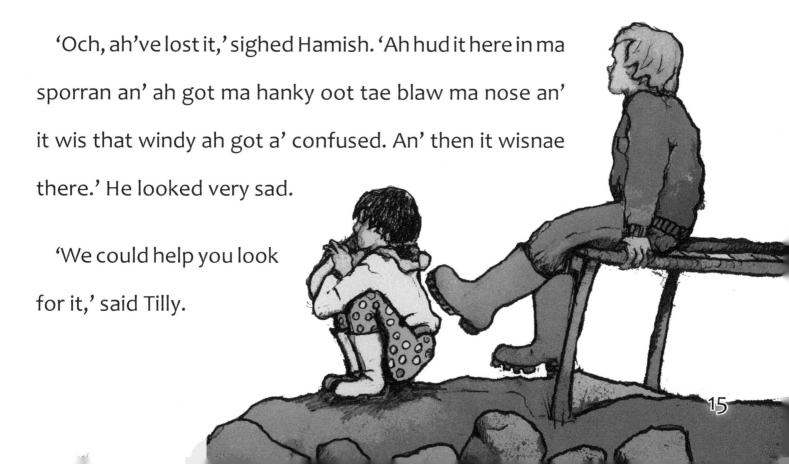

'You'll want to steal my treasure then,' said Hamish suspiciously.

The three children looked shocked. 'Who do you think we are?' asked Tilly. 'People who steal things?'

She looked very annoyed.

'Thieves?' Effie had a deep frown on her face.

'Robbers?' shouted Manny. He was really angry.

'Naw, naw, naw,' said Hamish. 'Ah'm sorry. Ah didnae mean that—ah spoke wi'oot thinkin'.'

'Okay. In future, think before you speak,' said Effie (her Mum had said that to her lots of times and she was very pleased to be able to say it to someone else). 'Now, let's look for the map.'

So they looked everywhere. In forests, up hills, down cliffs, on the beach till they were exhausted.

Eventually, they all sat down on a big flat rock feeling very hot and very miserable because there was no sign anywhere of the map. The sweat was running down Hamish's face and dripping off his beard onto his hairy chest. He was also smelling a bit. He went into his sporran and brought out a huge, very clean, tartan hanky and began to wipe his face.

Manny, Effie and Tilly looked at each other.

Effie turned to look at Hamish. 'Where do you keep your dirty washing?' she said.

'Whit?' asked Hamish in astonishment.

'Where?' said Manny. 'Have you got a dirty washing basket?'

'A whit?' asked Hamish again.

'Do you ever do a washing?' asked Tilly.

Hamish looked very insulted. 'Aye, of course ah dae. Ah dae it every June—even if ma claes dinnae need it.' he said proudly. 'We wis properly trained oan the pirate ships.'

'SO WHERE ARE YOUR DIRTY CLOTHES?' shouted Effie.

'Och, there's a wee pile near the beach ready for the washing soon. Ah think in aboot six weeks.'

'Take us!' shouted the children.

Hamish thought that they'd all gone mad but, as he'd already insulted them about the thieving thing, he didn't want to offend them again so—reluctantly—he took them to a disgusting pile of clothes that lay behind a rock on the beach.

The children looked at it and then Manny said, 'Well here goes,' and the three of them began to search through the clothes—but only with one hand each, because they were holding their noses with the other.

Hamish watched them in complete bewilderment. 'EEEUGH!' yelled Effie at last. 'I've found it!'

And she held up a big piece of paper that was covered in snot and other unmentionable things, but you could still see a great big cross on it.

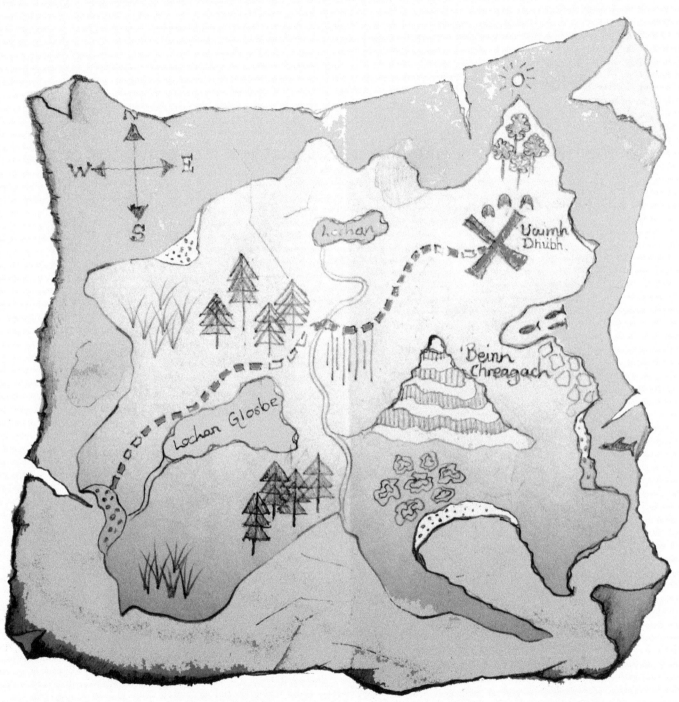

'Ma map!' shouted Hamish and he danced a jig in glee. 'Ye found it! Hoo did ye ken it wis there?'

'You'd used it instead of your hanky,' said Effie. 'You still had your hanky in your sporran.'

'Och aye! Whit a turnip-heid,' and Hamish laughed and laughed till his beard nearly fell off. 'Noo come awa an' we'll find the treasure.'

And once again, but this time following the map, they walked up hills, through forests and down cliffs, till they came to a cave with a great big cross on the floor.

'This is it!' shouted Hamish, and he began to dig with his knife in the sandy soil. The children helped using big bits of driftwood that were lying around the cave. Soon, they uncovered a huge pirate's chest. Hamish produced a key from his sporran and unlocked it but, instead of coins and jewels as the children had expected, there were only old books and bottles.

'Oh,' they sighed, disappointed, but not wanting to hurt Hamish's feelings as he was so delighted you'd have thought it was Christmas.

'What is it?' asked Effie.

'The books contain a' the wisdom from the auld folk—poems an' stories an' sangs—a' frae Scotland. And the bottles are *uisge-beatha*—the water of life—and they're very, very old.

'Can I have some?' asked Effie.

'Ach naw—it's no fur the wee ones, but ah huv a wee sip o' something fur ye.'

And he rummaged around in the bottom of the chest and brought out a bottle full of a beautiful golden liquid. 'Noo this is a wee drink jist for bairns who travel on tartan trampolines. It's meant to make ye strang. Ah think a wee sip'll get ye up in the air again.'

He gave them all a sip from the bottle and then shook their hands.

'Ah want tae thank yez all for yer help. If yez hudnae helped, mebbe a' these poems an' stories an' sangs wid huv been lost forever. It wis a happy day when yez landed on ma island an' ah hope yez'll a' come back soon.'

Manny and Effie and Tilly began to feel a wee bit dizzy, so they closed their eyes and—

—suddenly found themselves flying through the air again on the Tartan Trampoline.

'How the heck did that happen?' asked Effie as they looked down again on the lochs and mountains.

'No idea,' said Manny, 'but maybe that golden drink had something to do with it.'

'I think so,' said Tilly. 'It tasted a bit like iron.'

'Mmm.' said the others, and they all rolled over and watched the clouds sail by as the Tartan Trampoline took them towards home.

That was actually so great,' said Effie. The others laughed, but then gradually they all became very serious as a new thought occurred to them.

'What's Shayjay going to say?' said Tilly.

'We've been away for the whole day,' said Effie.

'She's probably called the police and the mountain rescue. I think we might be in real trouble,' said Manny.

The trampoline landed gently and the children climbed down.

They crossed the field very slowly and opened the door of the house fearfully—

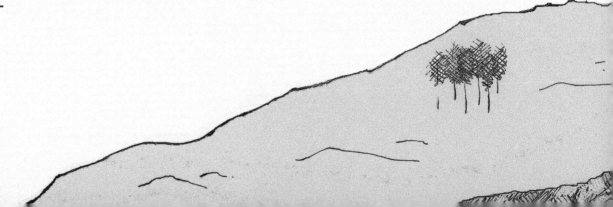

only to meet Shayjay coming down the stairs in her pyjamas and yawning widely.

'Oh good morning, my lovely children. Have you been out playing already? Come into the kitchen and we'll all have breakfast.'

The three looked at each other with huge grins.

'This surely is an enchanted island,' they all thought.

Acknowledgements

Many thanks to Arthur Cross, Bob Hay and Lorna MacKinnon who sowed the seeds of a great idea which Sarah Campbell and I immediately took up to produce this series of books.

The children of the island primary school 'road-tested' the stories and made valuable suggestions. Thanks, guys!

Thanks also to Adam Mahon, Ruben Campbell-Paine, Amy Bowman and Issy Budd who acted as models for some of the characters.

Lightning Source UK Ltd.
Milton Keynes UK
UKHW021143021221
394922UK00005B/83